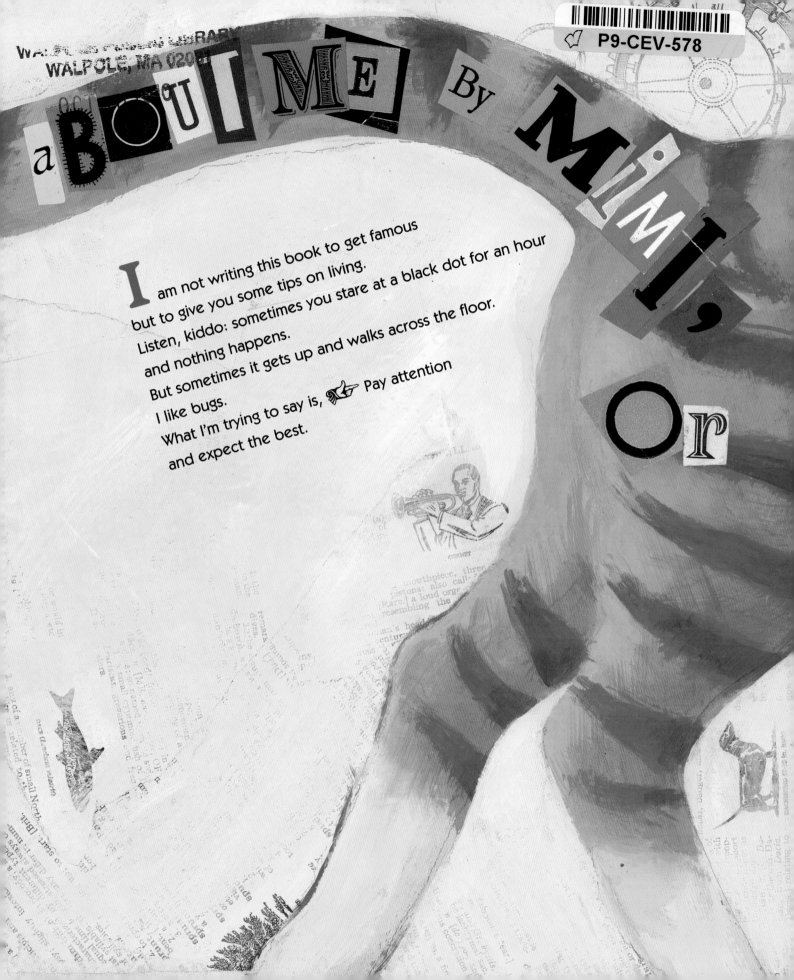

aBOUt ME By MiMI, Or

I am not writing this book to get famous
but to give you some tips on living.
Listen, kiddo: sometimes you stare at a black dot for an hour
and nothing happens.
But sometimes it gets up and walks across the floor.
I like bugs.
What I'm trying to say is, ☞ Pay attention
and expect the best.

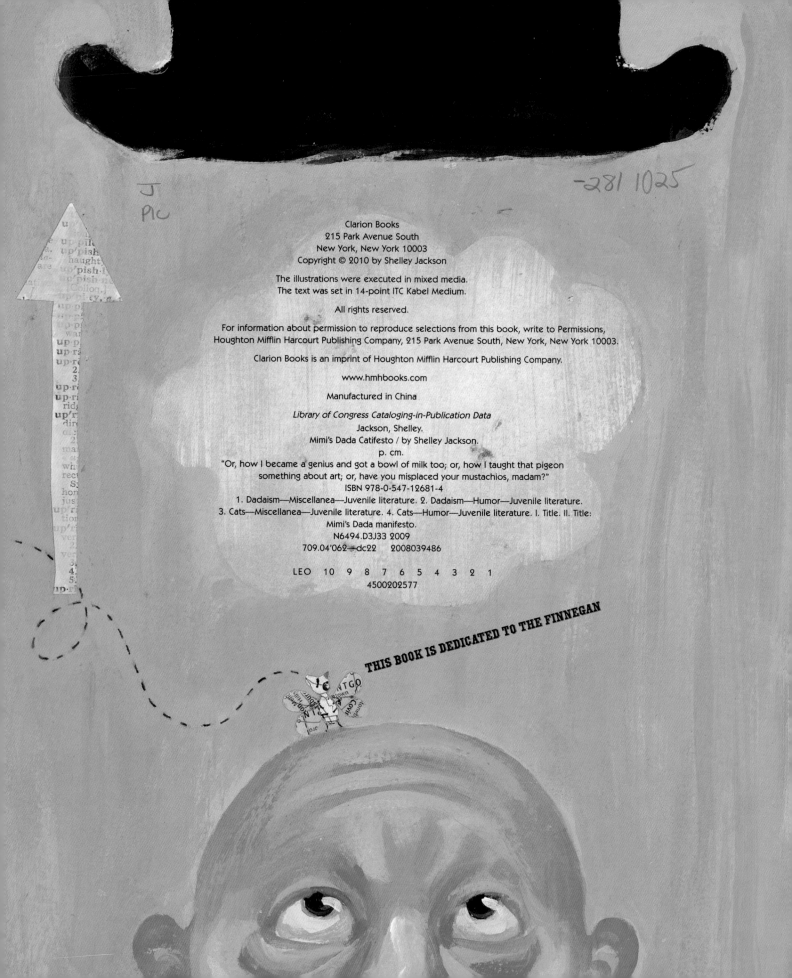

J
PIC

-281 1025

Clarion Books
215 Park Avenue South
New York, New York 10003
Copyright © 2010 by Shelley Jackson

The illustrations were executed in mixed media.
The text was set in 14-point ITC Kabel Medium.

For information about permission to reproduce selections from this book, write to Permissions,
Houghton Mifflin Harcourt Publishing Company, 215 Park Avenue South, New York, New York 10003.

Clarion Books is an imprint of Houghton Mifflin Harcourt Publishing Company.

www.hmhbooks.com

Manufactured in China

Library of Congress Cataloging-in-Publication Data
Jackson, Shelley.
Mimi's Dada Catifesto / by Shelley Jackson.
p. cm.
"Or, how I became a genius and got a bowl of milk too; or, how I taught that pigeon
something about art; or, have you misplaced your mustachios, madam?"
ISBN 978-0-547-12681-4
1. Dadaism—Miscellanea—Juvenile literature. 2. Dadaism—Humor—Juvenile literature.
3. Cats—Miscellanea—Juvenile literature. 4. Cats—Humor—Juvenile literature. I. Title. II. Title:
Mimi's Dada manifesto.
N6494.D3J33 2009
709.04'062—dc22   2008039486

LEO 10 9 8 7 6 5 4 3 2 1
4500202577

THIS BOOK IS DEDICATED TO THE FINNEGAN

YOU may be surprised to hear that I was once
a poor alley cat.
I lived in a hat that blew off a rich man's head.
I was lucky he had a big head.

There are many cats in Zurich
and many artists
but few artistic cats.
The others laughed at me.
"Get a human," they meowed. "It's easy.
1. purr,
2. look cute,
3. don't wash your behind while they're watching.
That's all humans want from us cats."
Well, that's not enough for Mimi.

My only friend was a cynical old pigeon, Laszlo.
"Humans have fireplaces, milk,
and laps. Think about it," he said.

"Humans? Noisy things
who can't even lick their own toes," I sneered.
"Do I look like a cat who comes running
to whoever coos **Kitty, kitty?**
For a cat with the soul of an artist,
only an artist will do."
(Of course, a bowl of milk would be nice
once in a while.)

One day I was slinking and strutting down a dark and crooked street, looking for something to eat. A small door stood open. Out of it came **yells, bangs, thumps,** and a thought-provoking smell. The smell was strange yet achingly familiar. Above all it was yummy. Obviously, I went in.

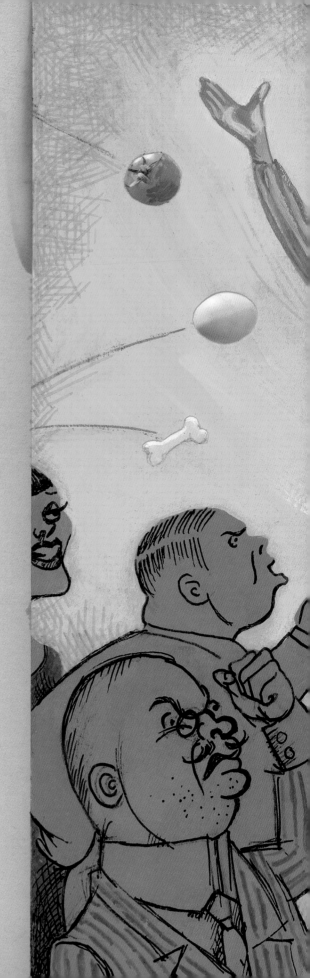

At the end of the room was a stage.
On the stage was a piano,
and on the piano was a man
with a pointy beard
and a coat made of paper.
He had a fish on top of his head.

The fish smelled dee-lish.
The man had taste,
and he could sing
almost as well as a cat:
"WAAAA! GA GA UMBA, UMBA PEE!"
The fish flopped this way and that.
It seemed to be smiling
right at me, kiddo.

It was a splendid performance.
The crowd threw gifts of food at the man—
chicken bones, tomatoes, eggs—
which made beautiful patterns on his coat.

"ART," the man cried, pulling a
drumstick out of his sleeve,
"is anything! Umbrellas! Bow ties! False teeth!
Only art that doesn't look like art is art!
GA GA UMBA, UMBA POO!"
At this the crowd threw so many gifts
that the artist hid under the piano.
I stretched my back in a bow.
        I was very moved.

When I sat up, the fish
was alone in the spotlight.

How beautiful!

I grabbed it and ran

down the dark street,

to the top of a fence,

up a flight of stairs,

THIS SIDE UP

over the roof
of an old shed,

and down a pile of cobblestones

"LASZLO! LASZLO!" I called.

to my hat.

A shoe flew
out a window.
Such marvels often happen
to cats like me.
I have a very large
collection of shoes.

Laszlo thumped down beside me.
"Must you make that noise?" he asked. "Nice fish."
I stretched out a trembling paw. "The fish," I said,
"is nothing! I, Mimi, have found my artist!"

"Oh yes?" said Laszlo, cleaning between his toes.
"Is he a cubist, a futurist, or an expressionist?
Does he paint guitars, airplanes, or women?"

"Only art that does not look like art is art," I said.

"Ah! He is a Dadaist," said Laszlo. "Poor Mimi.
That bowl of milk looks very far away."

"Milk? Hah!" I sniffed. "We will live for beauty,
Mr. Dada and I!"

The cockroaches giggled.

C _ _ _ _ _ t

F _ _ _ _ _ _ _

E _ p _ _ s s _ _ _ _ _ t

GRAPHIC CONTROLS CORPORATION
BUFFALO, NEW YORK

1854

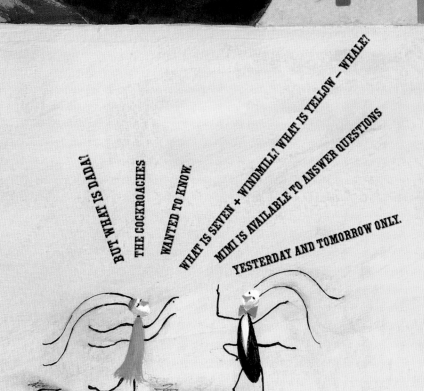

BUT WHAT IS DADA?
THE COCKROACHES
WANTED TO KNOW.
WHAT IS SEVEN + WINDMILL? WHAT IS YELLOW − WHALE?
MIMI IS AVAILABLE TO ANSWER QUESTIONS
YESTERDAY AND TOMORROW ONLY.

D _ _ _ _ _ _

At the next show, Mr. Dada held up an ice cube.
"Here is my latest sculpture," he said. "It is called

Mr. Lamp
has lost
Pudding his
clock"

The ice cube melted. The crowd roared.
Mr. Dada wiped his hands on his beard,
and left. I followed.

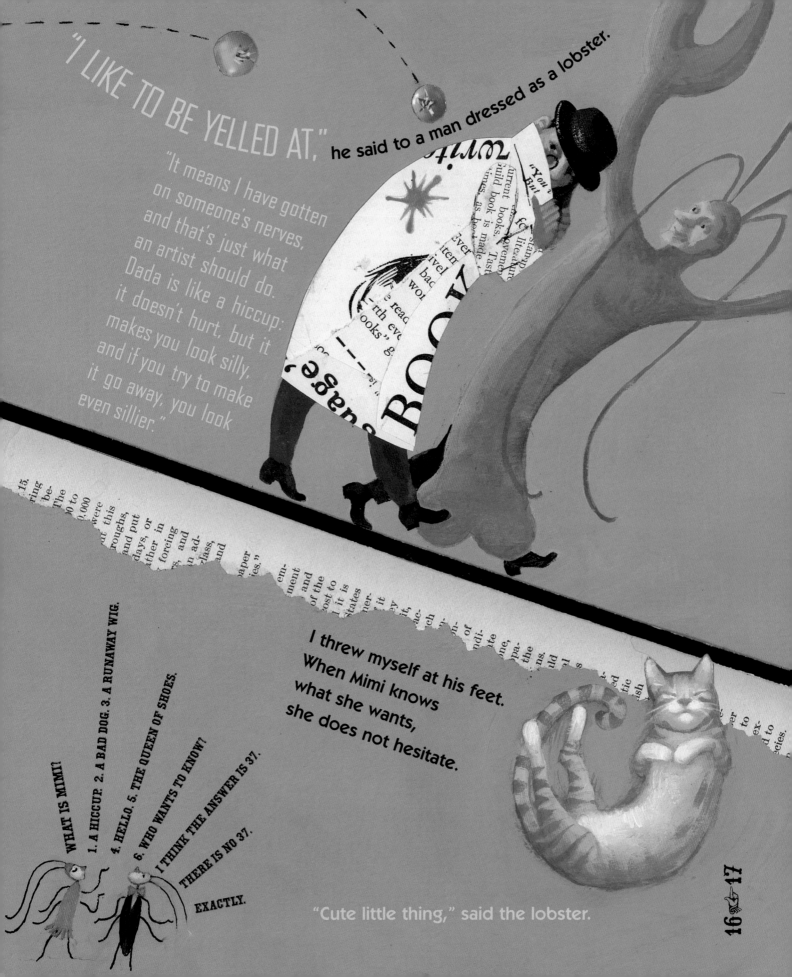

"I LIKE TO BE YELLED AT," he said to a man dressed as a lobster.

"It means I have gotten on someone's nerves, and that's just what an artist should do. Dada is like a hiccup: it doesn't hurt, but it makes you look silly, and if you try to make it go away, you look even sillier."

I threw myself at his feet.
When Mimi knows what she wants,
she does not hesitate.

WHAT IS MIMI?
1. A HICCUP. 2. A BAD DOG. 3. A RUNAWAY WIG.
4. HELLO. 5. THE QUEEN OF SHOES.
6. WHO WANTS TO KNOW?
I THINK THE ANSWER IS 37.
THERE IS NO 37.
EXACTLY.

"Cute little thing," said the lobster.

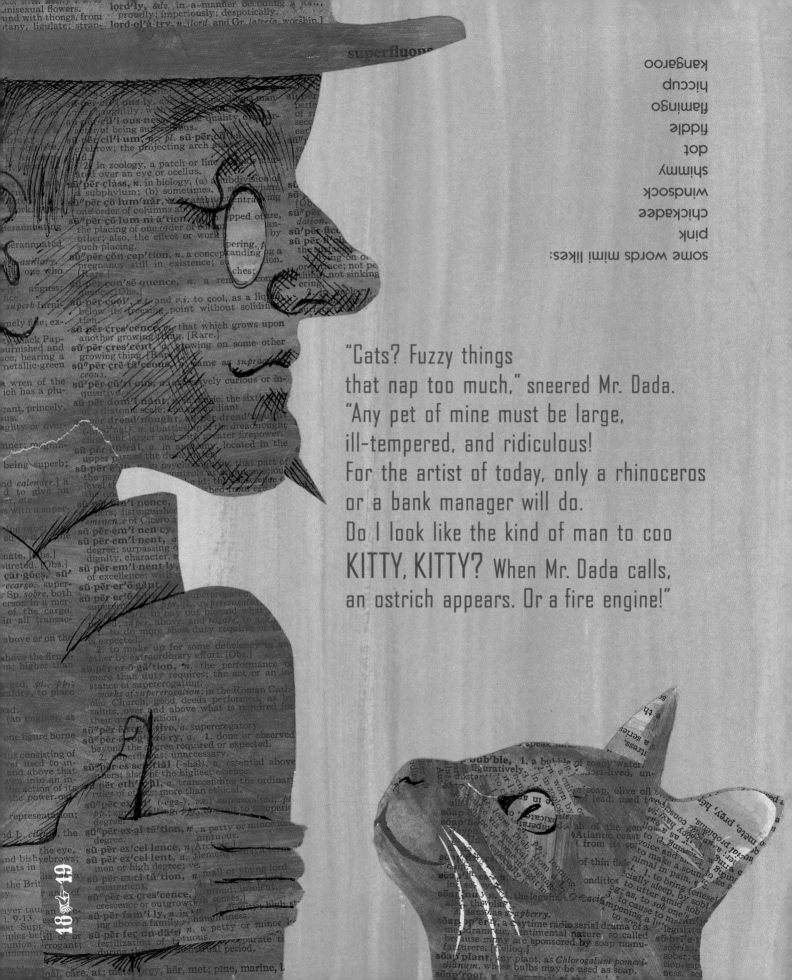

"Cats? Fuzzy things
that nap too much," sneered Mr. Dada.
"Any pet of mine must be large,
ill-tempered, and ridiculous!
For the artist of today, only a rhinoceros
or a bank manager will do.
Do I look like the kind of man to coo
KITTY, KITTY? When Mr. Dada calls,
an ostrich appears. Or a fire engine!"

"I will perform for him," I decided. "When he sees that I am a Dadaist too, he will take me in." I curled my tail around my legs and looked up at the sky for inspiration. After a minute, I began to sing.

"What is that awful noise?" asked Laszlo.

"Don't bother me, pigeon. I'm working," I said. "It is a sound poem."

"It's not very pretty," said Laszlo.

"It's not supposed to be pretty. It is mysterious and awe-inspiring."

"It doesn't mean anything," said Laszlo.

"It's not supposed to mean anything. It's a sound poem. You're just supposed to listen to it."

"No, thank you!" said Laszlo, flapping away.

Mimi says, Now perform a sound poem.

Yes, you.

Did I hear a burp?

Thank you—
that was a good poem.

Under the moon
from the top of the fence
outside Mr. Dada's window
I delivered my poem:

Mr. Dada opened his window.
I made up a few new lines on the spot.
They were not quite as good, but I
delivered them with feeling:

meee?

meer?

mEOW!

"SHOE!" said Mr. Dada,
and that is what he gave me.
Another shoe for my collection.

THE COCKROACHES
PERFORM A SOUND POEM:

XTTPPPPI IX:JX.

XJ!!SZZXT...PXI

"How were the reviews?" asked Laszlo.

"Encouraging," said I. "He threw a shoe."

"Ah," said Laszlo.

"It was a nice gesture," I said,
"but he should have been more careful."

"Didn't you duck?"

"That's the problem," I replied.
"The shoe went through a window
next door. I don't think his neighbor
appreciates Dada."

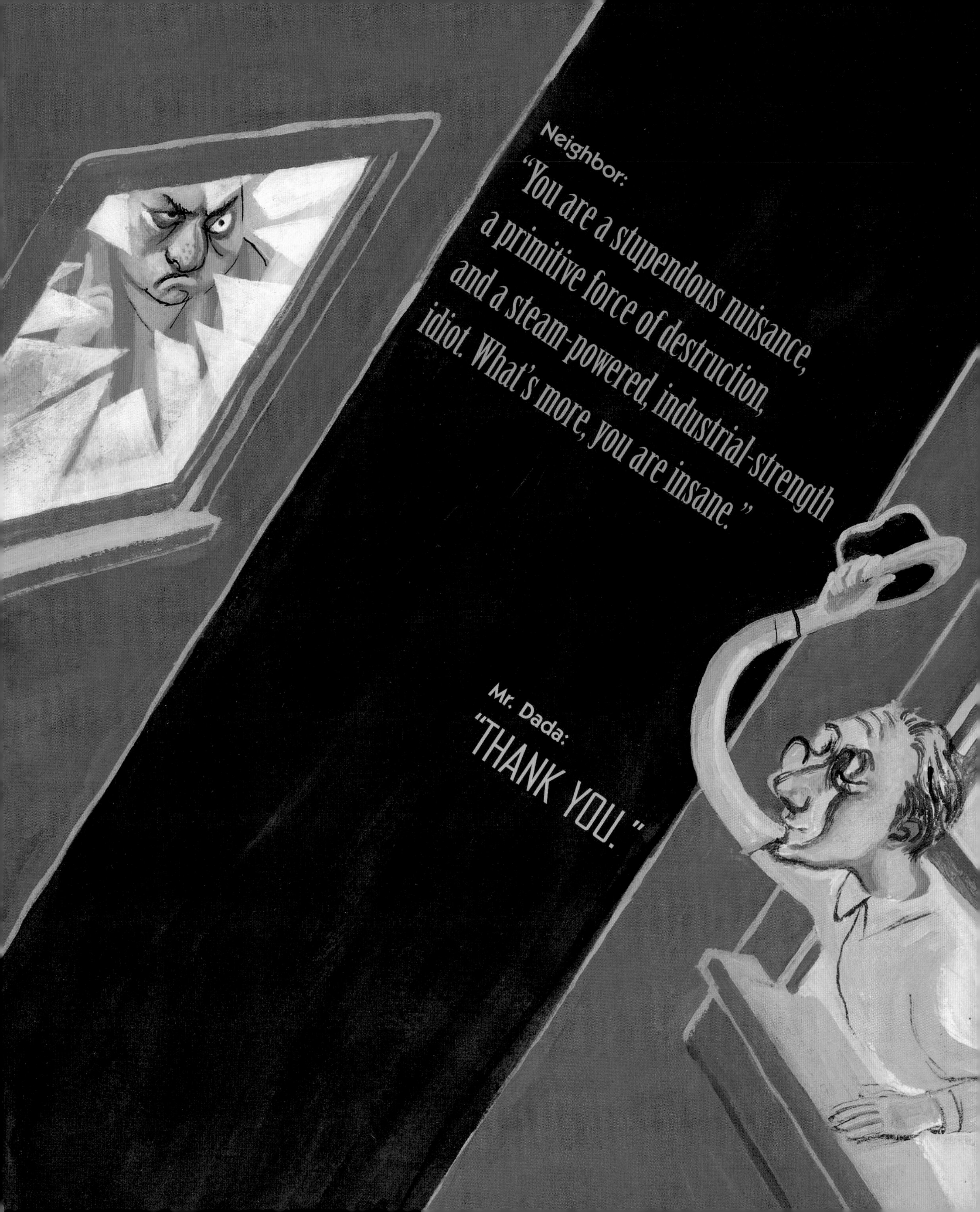
Neighbor:
"You are a stupendous nuisance,
a primitive force of destruction,
and a steam-powered, industrial-strength
idiot. What's more, you are insane."
Mr. Dada:
"THANK YOU."

I decided to have an art show in front of Mr. Dada's house.

Mimi's Gallery

a HAiRBall

A dead buG

~~another dead bug~~ LIVE!

SORRY, EXHIBIT CLOSED INDEFINITELY.

"Mimi," said Laszlo, "you didn't even make these yourself, except for the hairball."

"Laszlo, don't you know anything? These are called 'ready-mades' because they are already made. They are art because I say so. Look at that crumb— that's art too."

"Your best work," Laszlo said, and ate it.

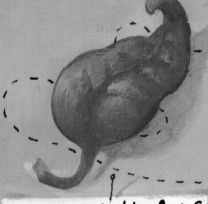

an ENiGMaticLEAf

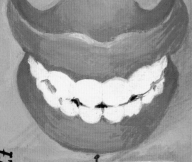

FALSe teeTh

A PAiNtiNG by LAsZlo

PiGEOn FOOt (WiTH CRUMB)

Gallery of

- - - - - - - - - -

[you.]

{

put your ready-made
right

HERE

}

Now for your art show! I can't wait!

What is it?

Beats me!

TRASH!

Just plain weird.

What do you mean, not for sale?

Bo!

I believe I
detect the
influence of
"Mimi."

Hmm.

GENIUS!

"Your ears are drooping," said Laszlo.
"Was the show a flop?"

"Laszlo, Mr. Dada swept up
my ready-mades
and threw them away!
In his art gallery, he puts
a toothpick on a pedestal,
but when I show my best hairball,
he mistakes it for trash!"

"Mimi," said Laszlo,
"you're a silly little mammal.
You're going about this all wrong.
Just sit on his stoop
and look fluffy.
Make like a **pet**.
Even a Dadaist
doesn't want a Dada cat."

dada

To make matters worse
Mr. and Mrs. Cockroach
were about to have children——
twenty or thirty of them.
They wanted to know if I would
vacate the premises.
Get out, in other words.
They were afraid an artist would be
a bad influence on the little ones.

I was discouraged.

I prayed to the moon for **luck.**

Luck deluxe: The window was open,
and Mr. Dada was out on the town.
There was a small fish in the kitchen, and I was hungry.
I confess I was tempted.
But there are more important things
than eating. I went to work.

dear

mr.

dada

ripped

up

diary

your

I have

write

this

and

used

your

words

of

poem

I have spilled
the peas
that were in
the glass bowl

and which
you were probably
saving for dinner

forgive me
they were magical
so smooth
and so round most of them
you will find

eventually

there are 37 peas on this page.
can you find them all?

I've turned your sweater back into yarn. Can you find the end?

TODAY, I AM MARCHING FOR:
BEETLES
BOUNCY BALLS
STRING
PENGUINS
DOG LEASHES
AND THE WORD

AND

Now make your own poem:
Cut words out of a newspaper,
put them in a bag—and shake.
Take them out one at a time—no peeking—
and write them down.
Mimi says that's how you make
a good poem . . .
and even better news.

Incredibly Great Poem
_____, Dadaist

by _____

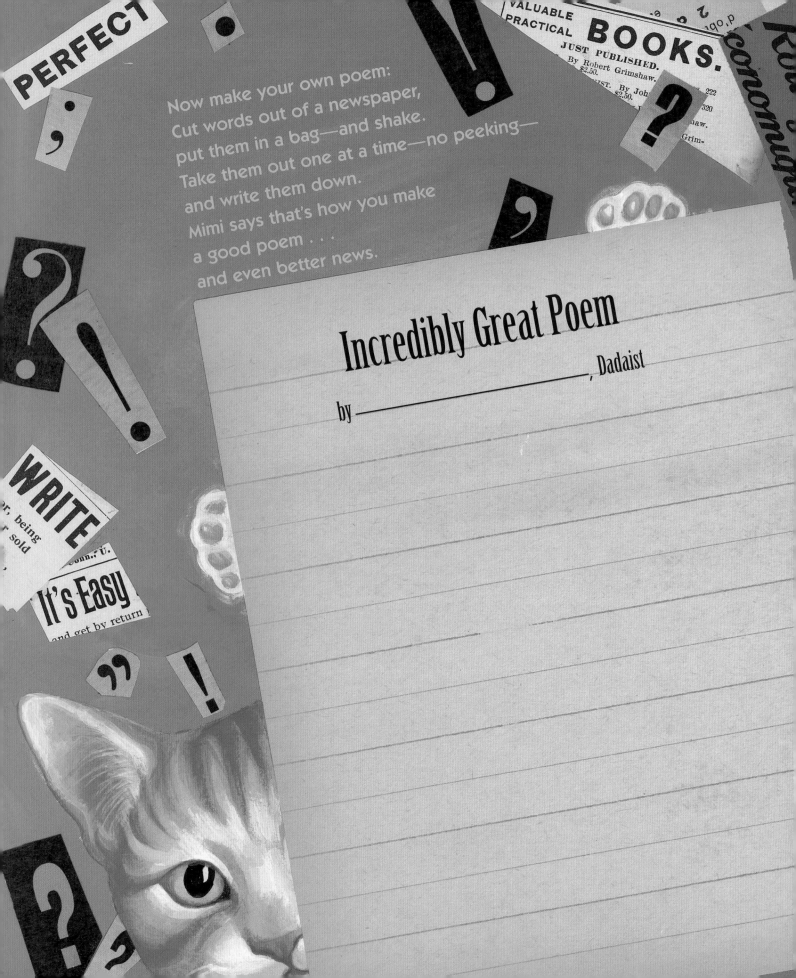

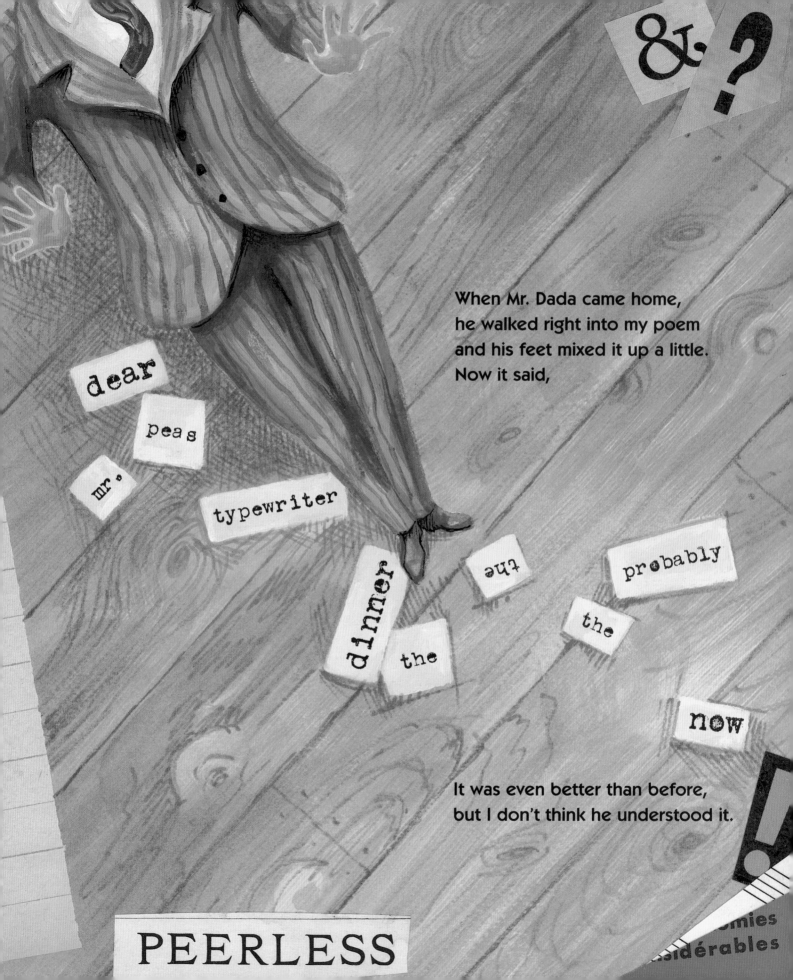

When Mr. Dada came home,
he walked right into my poem
and his feet mixed it up a little.
Now it said,

dear

peas

mr.

typewriter

dinner

the

the

probably

now

It was even better than before,
but I don't think he understood it.

PEERLESS

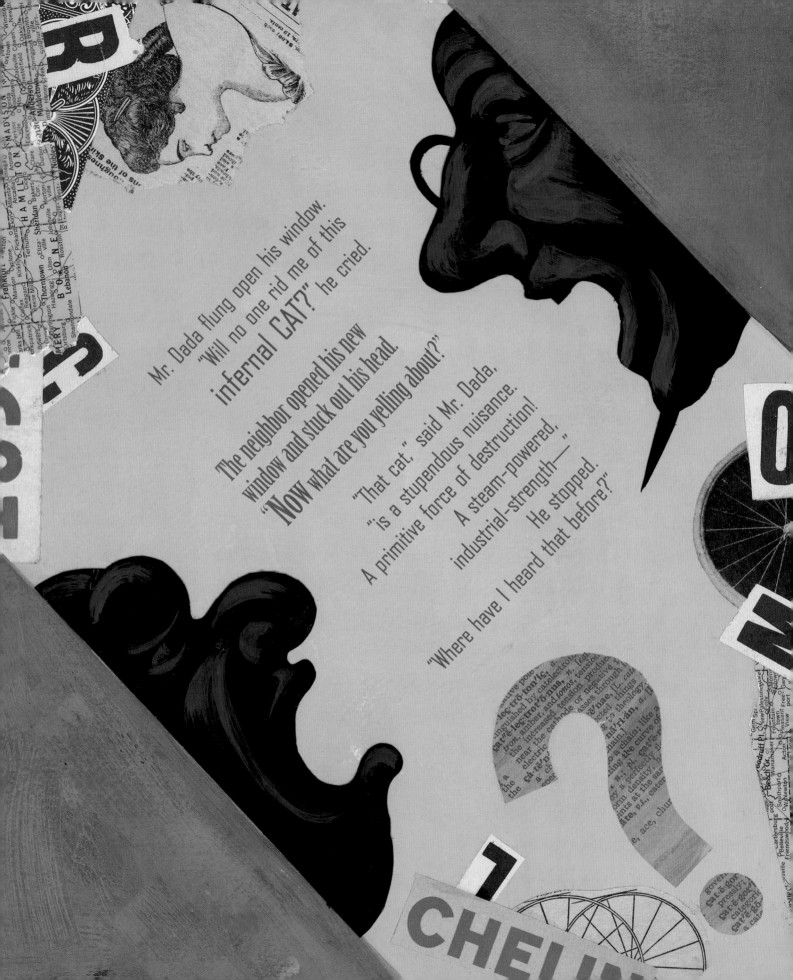

Mr. Dada flung open his window. "Will no one rid me of this infernal CAT?" he cried.

The neighbor opened his new window and stuck out his head. "Now what are you yelling about?"

"That cat," said Mr. Dada, "is a stupendous nuisance. A primitive force of destruction! A steam-powered, industrial-strength—" He stopped.

"Where have I heard that before?"

I balanced the fish on my head and made my best entrance.

The Dadaist looked at me.
"Oho," he said. "Hmm."

"At last you understand,"
said the neighbor.
"My windows are safe!"

"At last I understand," said Mr. Dada.
"I have met my equal! Together
we will create the world's
most astonishing—"

"MESS!" yelled the neighbor,
and slammed his window shut.

But we were not really listening.
I, Mimi, had found my human,
and at last
my human had found me.

A few weeks later I was
daydreaming over a bowl of milk
when Laszlo crash-landed beside me.
I was so pleased to see him, I got hiccups.

"You're getting fat," he said.

Chiccup "Don't hiccup me," I purred. "I'm thinking
about cookies and kangaroos,
the squash and the squid,
and all the little cockroaches
playing in my hat.
hiccup
I'm so happy,
if I were a dress, I'd have ruffles!"

"You're not turning up your nose
at a bowl of milk now. What about art?"

I sniffed. "Don't you understand, pigeon?
A bowl of milk is art.
A hiccup is art.
And you are art, even though
you look like a feather duster. Maybe especially
because you look like a feather duster!
Art can be anything.
GA GA UMBA, UMBA POO!"

WHAT IS DADA?

AUTHOR'S NOTE

Wearing a sock on your elbow is Dada. Spinning in circles and shouting "Salami!" is Dada. Sneezing is definitely Dada. Dada is anything silly and surprising.

Dada was "invented" in 1915 in Zurich, Switzerland. (Or maybe in Berlin or Paris—Dadaists like to argue.) The world was full of silly things in 1915, just like now (umbrellas! bow ties! false teeth!), but most art ignored the silliness. To the Dadaists, that was the silliest thing of all.

The Dadaists thought it was time to make art just as silly as the real world. They performed nonsense poems. They wore funny costumes. They put ordinary things like neckties and toilets in museums as if they were pieces of art. They parodied things that other people took very seriously, such as political speeches, money, and war.

Some people who went to their shows felt that they were being teased or cheated. They were angry! Some people laughed. And some said to themselves, Maybe toilets and neckties really *are* just as interesting as paintings and sculptures, if you look carefully.

Nobody could agree about what Dada meant, and nobody really understood Dada—not even Dadaists! Some people would be discouraged by this, but not the Dadaists. They thought that when you understand something, you stop thinking about it. *Not* understanding is much more interesting.

The Dadaists made art out of everything. Pieces of newspapers, ads, junk they found on the street—even other works of art. One of Marcel Duchamp's best-known artworks is a copy of a very famous painting by Leonardo da Vinci, of a lady called Mona Lisa. He made two changes: He gave her a mustache and a little pointed beard.

This is a Dadaist book, and so, like the Dadaists, I borrowed from many famous works of art to make it.

Mimi herself was inspired by a book I loved when I was a kid, called *Archy and Mehitabel*. It's about a poetic cockroach and his cat friend. The book was written by Don Marquis and illustrated by the great cartoonist George Herriman, who also invented a character called Krazy Kat—definitely a relative of Mimi's.

The idea of writing a *CAT*ifesto was inspired by Tristan Tzara's *Seven Dada Manifestos*. Many modern artists wrote manifestos in which they laid out the principles of their work in very serious language. But Tzara's manifestos were different. They poked fun at the very idea of manifestos. They were part poem, part picture, part nonsense. So I thought, Why not part story, too?

My pictures are inspired by many different artists, especially John Heartfield and Hannah Höch, who glued scraps of photographs together to make surprising new pictures, and Kurt Schwitters, who made things out of junk he found on the street.

Mimi's art show was inspired by Marcel Duchamp, who invented the "ready-made."

Mimi's sound poem was inspired by those of Hugo Ball, Kurt Schwitters, and Raoul Hausmann.

Mimi's writing was inspired by Tristan Tzara, who invented a new way to write poetry by cutting up a newspaper and pulling the pieces out of a bag. Her poem about peas is an homage to a poem about plums by William Carlos Williams called "This Is Just to Say."

I don't know if the Dadaists ever made art out of ice cubes, but later on an artist named Allan Kaprow did, in a sculpture called *Fluids*. His ice cubes were the size of bricks!

The neighbor who tells Mr. Dada, "What's more, you are insane," is quoting a great novel by Vladimir Nabokov called *Pale Fire*.

The costumes of Mr. Dada and his friend are inspired by Hugo Ball's costumes. He really did wear a pair of giant lobster claws. However, I don't think any Dadaist actually wore a fish on his head, because it would be very difficult to do. You try it! Fish are slippery!

Above all, I was inspired by a cat I once had, named Hen. Many cats are Dadaists. Do you know one?

MORE ABOUT DADA

Books

Dickerman, Leah, et al. *Dada: Zurich, Berlin, Hanover, Cologne, New York, Paris.* New York: Distributed Art Publishers/The National Gallery of Art, 2005.

Gale, Matthew. *Dada and Surrealism.* London: Phaidon Press, 1997.

Hemus, Ruth. *Dada's Women.* New Haven, Conn.: Yale University Press, 2009.

Huelsenbeck, Richard. *The Dada Almanac.* Translated by Barbara Wright and James Kirkup. Atlas Press, 1994.

Motherwell, Robert, editor. *The Dada Painters and Poets: An Anthology.* Cambridge, Mass.: Belknap Press of Harvard University Press, 1989.

Richter, Hans. *Dada: Art and Anti-art.* Translated by David Britt. London: Thames and Hudson, 1997.

Tzara, Tristan. *Seven Dada Manifestos and Lampisteries.* Waterloo, U.K.: Calder Publications, 1981.

Websites

Electronic Poetry Center: Sound Poetry
http://epc.buffalo.edu/sound/soundpoetry.html

The International Dada Archive
www.lib.uiowa.edu/dada/index.html

National Gallery of Art: Dada Exhibition
www.nga.gov/exhibitions/2006/dada/cities/index.shtm

Ubuweb Sound: Dada for Now
www.ubu.com/sound/dada.html

Audio CDs

Arp, Hans, Raoul Hausmann, and Kurt Schwitters. *Dada/Antidada/Merz.* Brussels, Belgium: Sub Rosa, 2005.

Arp, Hans, and Marcel Duchamp, et al. *Voices of Dada.* Norfolk, U.K.: LTM, 2006.